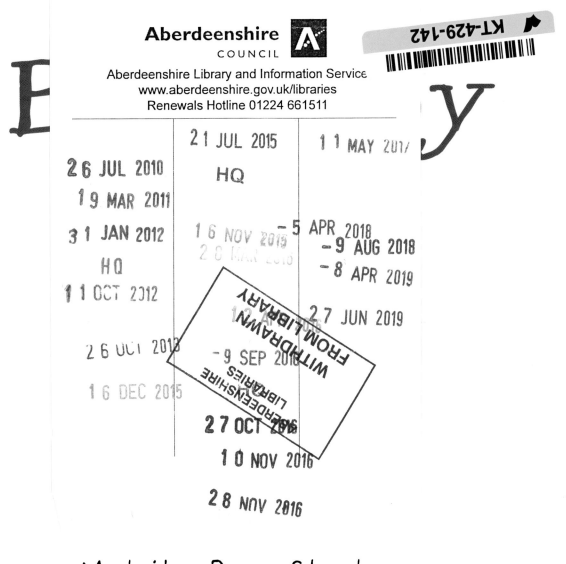

Malaika Rose Stanley

Illustrated by

Ken Wilson-Max

BABY RUBY BAWLED
TAMARIND BOOKS 978 1 848 53017 1
Published in Great Britain by Tamarind Books,
a division of Random House Children's Books
A Random House Group Company

This edition published 2010

1 3 5 7 9 10 8 6 4 2



TAMARIND BOOKS
61–63 Uxbridge Road, London, W5 5SA

www.**tamarindbooks**.co.uk
www.**kidsatrandomhouse**.co.uk
www.**rbooks**.co.uk
Addresses for companies within The Random House Group Limited can be found at:
www.**randomhouse**.co.uk/offices.htm

THE RANDOM HOUSE GROUP Limited Reg. No. 954009

A CIP catalogue record for this book is available from the British Library.

Printed and bound in China

For Letiya and Joel

and in loving memory of Jo and Helen

M.R.S.

For Jessica

K.W.M.

Theo loved his little sister, Ruby,
but there was one **BIG** problem.

Baby Ruby would not sleep.

She would not sleep at nap-time.
She would not sleep at bed-time.
She would not sleep at any time at all.

Baby Ruby's family tried everything.

But Baby Ruby bawled.

She would not go to sleep.

Dad gave Ruby a bath.
Theo played splishy-sploshy
with her.

Baby Ruby laughed.
"All clean and sparkly,"
said Dad.

But when Dad put her into the cot...
Baby Ruby bawled!

Dad called Mum.

Mum came as fast
as she could.
She fed Ruby.

But when Mum put her
into the cot...
Baby Ruby bawled.

Mum sent
a text message
to Nana.

Nana came as fast as she could.
She drove round and round the block
till her head hurt.
But still Baby Ruby bawled.

Nana phoned Grandad.

Grandad came as fast as he could.
Theo and Grandad strolled round the garden.
"Snug as a bug in a rug," said Grandad.

But still
Baby Ruby bawled.

Mum, Dad and Theo took Ruby to see the doctor.
The doctor listened to her heart.
She looked in her ears and in her eyes.
She looked up Ruby's nose.
"Fit as a fiddle," said the doctor.

On the way home, Baby Ruby fell asleep!
"Marvellous!" Mum said.
"We can all have a sleep. That's just what we need."
"You wish!" thought Theo.

They carried Ruby upstairs and put
her into her cot…
Baby Ruby bawled!

Dad phoned Uncle Clyde.
Uncle Clyde came
as fast as he could.

He held Ruby in his arms
and rocked her gently.
He told her once-upon-a-time stories.

Baby Ruby bawled.

So, he rocked her quickly and
told Theo hairy-scary stories.
But still Baby Ruby bawled.

Uncle Clyde put Ruby in the buggy.
He pushed her backwards and
forwards till his arms ached.
But when Uncle Clyde
put her into the cot...

Baby Ruby bawled.

Then Theo had an idea.
"Listen up, Ruby," he shouted.
"Enough's enough!"
Ruby stared.
Theo began to sing.

Hush now, Ruby, don't you cry.
I will sing a lullaby.

Theo took a deep breath.
He went on singing.

Hush now, Ruby, rest your head.
We all need to go to bed.

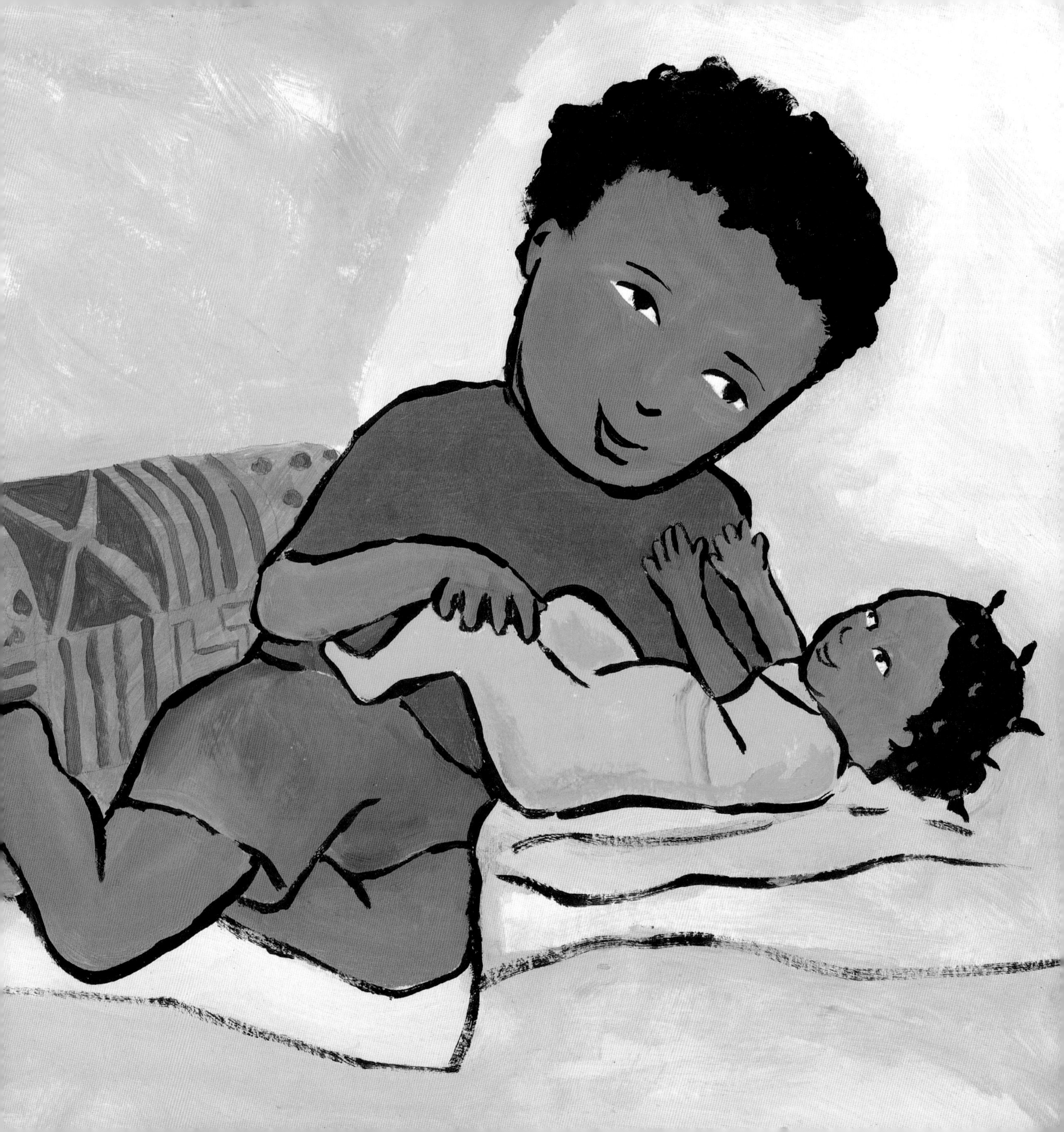

Theo was so tired,
he fell asleep
right there and
then and...

Baby Ruby said nothing at all.

# OTHER TAMARIND TITLES

## FOR READERS OF *Baby Ruby Bawled*

And Me!
Purrfect!
The Best Blanket
The Best Home
The Best Mum
The Best Toy
Let's Feed the Ducks
Let's Go to Bed
Let's Have Fun
Let's Go to Playgroup
I Don't Eat Toothpaste Anymore

## BOOKS FOR WHEN YOU GET A LITTLE OLDER...

The Silence Seeker
My Big Brother JJ
Siddharth and Rinki
Danny's Adventure Bus
Big Eyes, Scary Voices
The Night the Lights Went Out
Choices, Choices...
What Will I Be?
All My Friends
A Safe Place
Dave and the Tooth Fairy